Fairy Diddle

An Appalachian Fairy Tale

Karen Peters

Illustrated by Alyssa Rose

Archway Publishing books may be ordered through booksellers or by contacting:

Archway Publishing
1663 Liberty Drive
Bloomington, IN 47403
www.archwaypublishing.com
844-669-3957

Interior Image Credit: Alyssa Rose

ISBN: 978-1-6657-1430-3 (sc)
ISBN: 978-1-6657-1429-7 (e)

Print information available on the last page.

Archway Publishing rev. date: 11/19/2021

"Sit still! You're nothing but a fairy diddle!" Granny fussed as she brushed my damp, windswept hair. I was used to hearing her good-natured grumbling so it didn't make me as angry as it did when I was younger.

"We're having company for supper and I'll not have you looking like a ragamuffin!" Granny struggled to catch up a stray wisp of hair that refused to become part of the ponytail she was finishing while I continued to fidget.

"Granny, what's a fairy diddle?" Once more I got the answer I always heard.

"It's a twisty-turny, fidgety-feisty child that can't be still," she answered with a twinkle in her eyes.

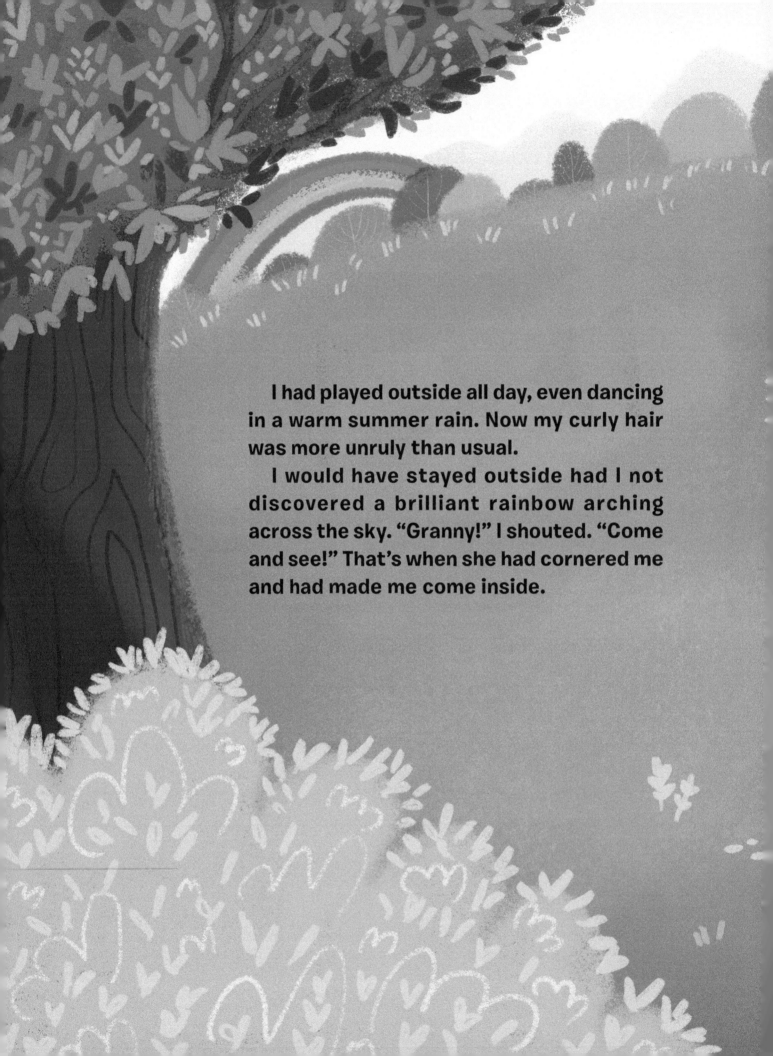

I had played outside all day, even dancing in a warm summer rain. Now my curly hair was more unruly than usual.

I would have stayed outside had I not discovered a brilliant rainbow arching across the sky. "Granny!" I shouted. "Come and see!" That's when she had cornered me and had made me come inside.

"But what IS a fairy diddle, REALLY, Granny?" I replied. "Tell me what it is really!"

"That's all it is and nothing more. You'll understand some day when you're a granny and pestered by children who can't sit still." She took one last stroke through the ponytail before I scooted off the stool and out the back door.

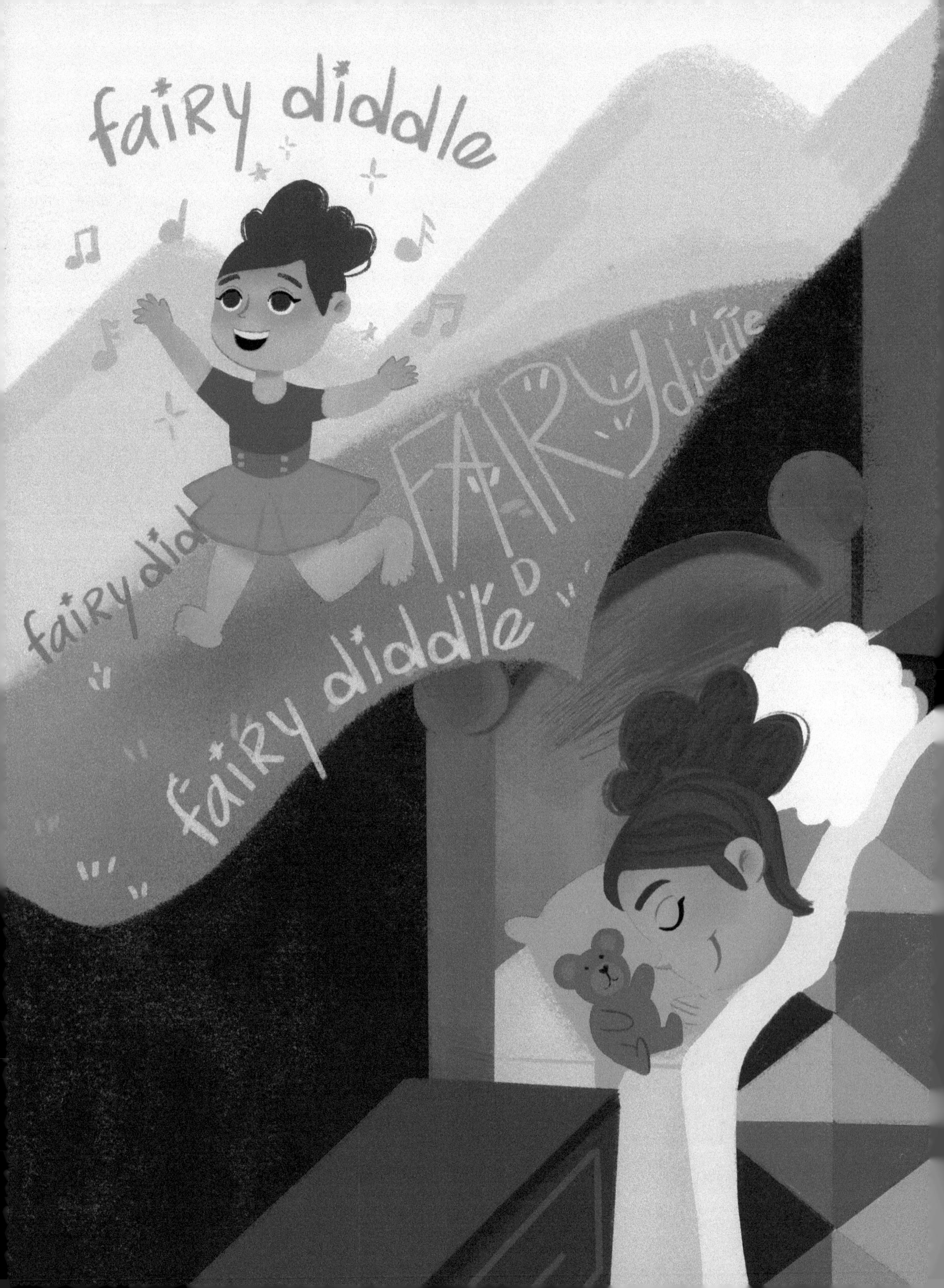
fairy diddle
fairy did
FAIRY diddle
fairy diddle

"Fairy diddle, fairy diddle, fairy diddle!" I sang as I skipped and ran and played. I liked the sound of the words even if I didn't know what they meant. I suspected my granny didn't know either. Maybe she had even made the words up.

That night I went to bed with all kinds of dreams in my head. As I cuddled against my granny's back, I remember wishing out loud, "Just once—that's all. Just one time, I wish I could meet a real live fairy diddle. I'd never squirm again."

Suddenly a silky golden light bathed the room and silvery tinkling music filled the air. Sparkly bits of red and green and blue and pink and purple and yellow swirled around my bed. Although I felt like I was in the middle of a wonderful, magical dream, I knew I was wide awake.

The light dimmed, the music stopped, and the pieces of color, as if by magic, molded together—red to red, green to green—and shapes of living things appeared. They gathered around my bed and waited for me to speak.

"W-w-what are y-y-you?" I stammered.

"We, my little lady, are fairy diddles!" boomed a gigantic red creature, his golden eyes blazing. "Couldn't you tell?"

"W-w-why n-n-no!" I replied. "I've never met a fairy diddle before. But could you be a little quieter? If you wake up my granny, she'll be furious."

"No, she won't!" boomed the red creature again. "You see, she can't hear us—or see us. No grownup can because they don't believe in us. Only believers can do that…. You are a believer, aren't you?" He leaned down and frowned suspiciously.

"Oh, yes!" I answered quickly. "At least I think so…."

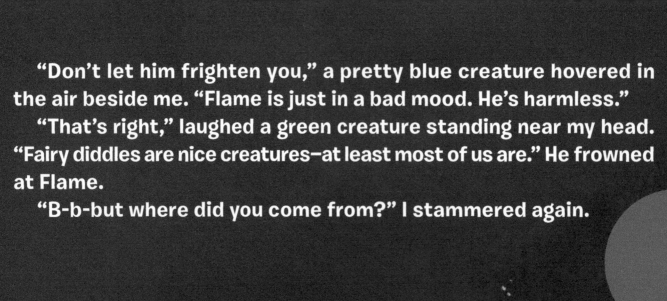

"Don't let him frighten you," a pretty blue creature hovered in the air beside me. "Flame is just in a bad mood. He's harmless."

"That's right," laughed a green creature standing near my head. "Fairy diddles are nice creatures—at least most of us are." He frowned at Flame.

"B-b-but where did you come from?" I stammered again.

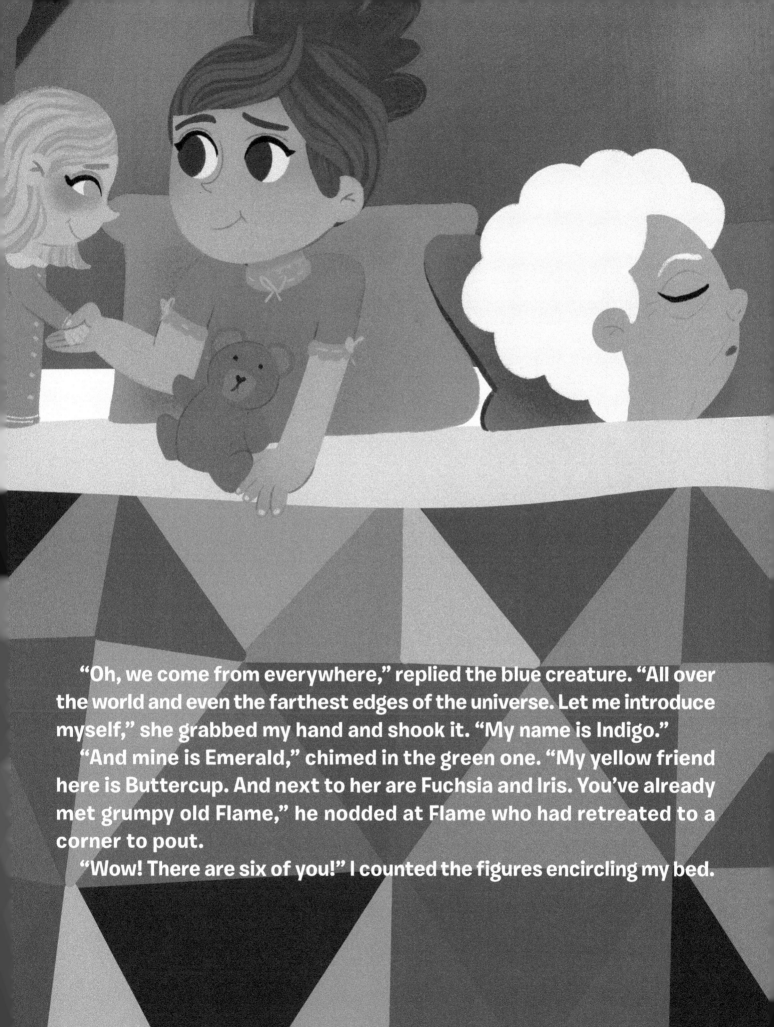

"Oh, we come from everywhere," replied the blue creature. "All over the world and even the farthest edges of the universe. Let me introduce myself," she grabbed my hand and shook it. "My name is Indigo."

"And mine is Emerald," chimed in the green one. "My yellow friend here is Buttercup. And next to her are Fuchsia and Iris. You've already met grumpy old Flame," he nodded at Flame who had retreated to a corner to pout.

"Wow! There are six of you!" I counted the figures encircling my bed.

"Actually, there are thousands of us," laughed Emerald and the others laughed, too. "There are fairy diddles all over the world at this very minute doing the jobs they were given to do."

"Ebony had to stay outside and weave the night," explained Buttercup. "He's as black as the darkest night. I'm here because the sun is in China right now and my cousin Goldenrod is weaving it."

"And Snowflake couldn't come because she had to spin a snowstorm for a penguin party at the South Pole," chimed in Iris.

I was beginning to understand. "You mean fairy diddles make colors?" I asked.

"You guessed it!" boomed Flame, a big smile spreading across his face. "That makes fairy diddles special," he boasted as the others nodded in agreement. "You see, I color the roses and the redbirds, the sunset and sometimes—when a rainstorm is coming—even the sunrise."

"And I paint the sky and the sea, and Emerald dyes the grass and the trees." Indigo added proudly. "Iris and Fuchsia take care of most of the flowers and help Flame with the long summer sunsets."

"We're around all the time," explained Fuchsia. "Most people just don't realize it."

"We're pretty much TOP SECRET!" boasted Iris. "But sometimes when a child is very special, we let him—or her, in your case—in on our secret."

"You see, we just had a special meeting and voted on you late this afternoon," whispered Buttercup.

"This afternoon? I don't understand...." I had so many questions I didn't know where to begin.

"Do you remember the warm rain you played in just before supper?" asked Indigo.

"Yes, but..." I began.

"Well, what did you see just as the sun peeped from behind the clouds?" Indigo grinned as I realized what she was asking.

"A rainbow!" I exclaimed. All my questions about fairy diddles were finally being answered in the most magical way!

"That's right," nodded Indigo. "Every time you see a rainbow, fairy diddles from all over the world are meeting to select another special girl or boy to share our secret."

"And every time you pick a flower or lie in the fresh green grass and watch the clouds float across the sky.... every time you swim in the sea or play in the snow or watch a sunset, you are surrounded by us—your friends!" smiled Flame warmly.

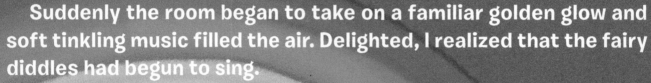

Suddenly the room began to take on a familiar golden glow and soft tinkling music filled the air. Delighted, I realized that the fairy diddles had begun to sing.

"Ringly, jingly, tingly toe-day is coming, and we must go!
Rumbly, bumbly, fumbly fiddles—we paint the world—we're FAIRY DIDDLES!"

As they sang their magical song, the fairy diddles joined hands and danced around my bed. They danced slowly at first, then faster and faster and FASTER until they dissolved into a blur of bright sparkly color.

Once more, the room was bathed in a silky golden glow and their singing melted into the familiar silvery music I had heard earlier. And then they were gone!

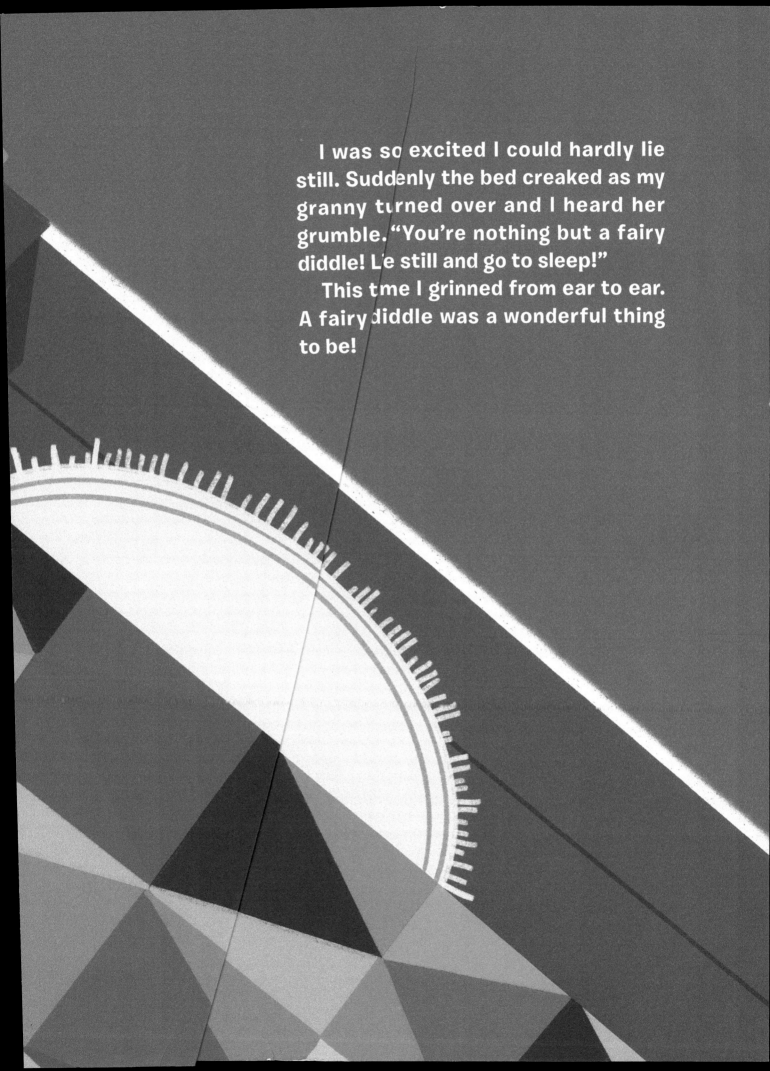

I was so excited I could hardly lie still. Suddenly the bed creaked as my granny turned over and I heard her grumble. "You're nothing but a fairy diddle! Lie still and go to sleep!"

This time I grinned from ear to ear. A fairy diddle was a wonderful thing to be!

CPSIA information can be obtained
at www.ICGtesting.com
Printed in the USA
BVHW020817060122
625448BV00034B/875

9 781665 714303